Meet Diego!

adapted by Leslie Valdes
based on the script by Eric Weiner
illustrated by Susan Hall

SCHOLASTIC INC.
New York   Toronto   London   Auckland   Sydney
Mexico City   New Delhi   Hong Kong   Buenos Aires

Based on the TV series *Dora the Explorer*® as seen on Nick Jr.®

ISBN 0-439-53929-3

12 11 10 9 8 7 6 5 4 3 2 1   3 4 5 6 7 8/0

Printed in the U.S.A.

First Scholastic printing, November 2003

¡Hola! I'm Dora, and this is my friend, Boots. We're at the Animal Rescue Center, where they help all kinds of animals.

Eeep, eeep!

Errr, errr!

I hear a sound. Look—Baby Bear is about to fall out of the tree! Hang on, Baby Bear! Oh, no—he's falling!

Meow, meow!

Here comes my cousin, Diego. He's saving Baby Bear. Wow!
Diego's really cool. He can make animal noises and talk to wild
animals.

Can you say "Errrr, errrr!" to Baby Bear?

Uh-oh! Someone's calling for help. Diego's field journal helps him identify animals. Let's check it to figure out who's calling for help.

It's Baby Jaguar, and he's in trouble! We've got to get to the waterfall to help him!

Map says that to get to Baby Jaguar we need to go through the rain forest and past the cave, and that's how we'll get to the waterfall. Will you help us save Baby Jaguar? We have to hurry! *¡Vámonos!*

We made it to the rain forest! Look—there's a zip cord! We can ride the zip cord through the treetops and zip through the rain forest.

Do *you* see a ladder we can climb up?
Oh, no! The ladder is missing six rungs. Let's find the rungs.

Thanks for helping fix the ladder. Now let's go save Baby Jaguar. Wheee!

We made it to the cave! Do you see a polar bear?
Diego's journal says polar bears live only in the cold. But it's really, really hot in the rain forest. . . .

Oh, no! That's not a polar bear! Do you know who it is? It's Swiper, that sneaky fox. He'll try to swipe Diego's journal. We have to say "Swiper, no swiping!" Say it with me: "Swiper, no swiping!"

Thanks for helping us stop Swiper! Now we need to find the waterfall. We can use Diego's spotting scope to see things that are far away!

There's the waterfall. . . . And there's Baby Jaguar!
We're coming, Baby Jaguar!

We can water-ski down the river to save Baby Jaguar.
Diego says if we ask the dolphin, he'll pull us through the water.
Can you help me call the dolphin? Say "Click, click!" Again!

Click, click!

The dolphin can pull us through the river, but we need something to hold on to. Let's check Backpack! Say "Backpack!" What can the dolphin use to pull us along the water?

A rope! *¡Excelente!* We all need to hold on to the rope. Put your hands out in front of you and hold on tight. Whoaaaa!

Yeah! We made it to the other side of the river.
   Oh, no! Baby Jaguar is about to fall over the giant waterfall!
Diego says the big condors can help us: They can fly us all the way
to Baby Jaguar. Say "Squawk, squawk!" to call the big condors!

squawk, squawk!

Quick! You have to help us fly to Baby Jaguar!
Flap your arms. Faster!

Hooray! We caught him!

We saved Baby Jaguar, and now the whole Jaguar family is together again. Thanks for helping!